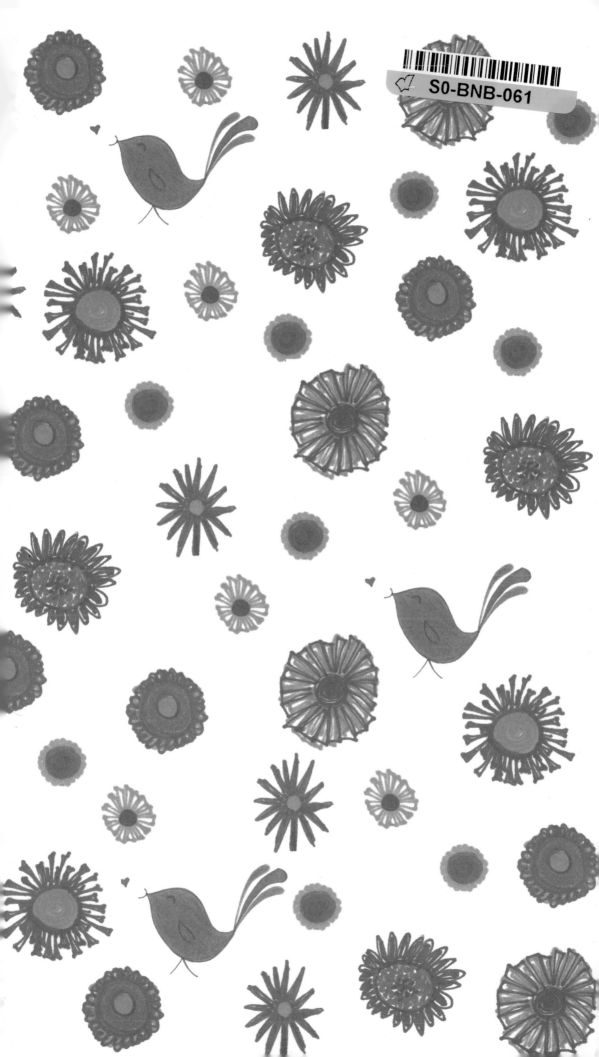

# Too Tall Alice

Written by Susie Sims Irvin

Illustrated by Melinda Dabbs

To the dearest of friends,
Sarah and Joe Little,
and two beautiful books!
7/10/08
Susie Sims Irvin

# Too Tall Alice

Copyright © 2007 by O'More Publishing
ISBN-10    0-9800285-3-1
ISBN-13    978-0-9800285-3-9

Written by Susie Sims Irvin
Illustrated by Melinda Dabbs
Art Direction by Jessa Rose Sexton
Layout and Typesetting by Paula Rozelle Bagnall

Published by:
O'More Publishing
A Division of O'More College of Design
423 South Margin St.
Franklin, TN 37064 U.S.A

# Dedication

To children.
 –Susie Sims Irvin

To all those dear to me who inspired the children in this book.
To my sweet love, Roger, for making the flowers bloom in my heart.
 –Melinda Dabbs


Community Childcare of Franklin, Tennessee,
a licensed, loving caregiver for children of working,
lower income families, will be the recipient of proceeds from this book,
as requested by the author, who is a founder of this program.

O'MORE
PUBLISHING
HISTORIC FRANKLIN,
TENNESSEE

Once upon a time
there was a little girl
named Alice.

Only she wasn't very little
for very long.

She outgrew her bassinet

her walker

and her stroller.

Her mother couldn't keep her in clothes.

And when she started to school
they always put Alice
at the very back of the line.

"Where are we going, Alice?"
the children asked.
Because Alice could stand
at the back of the line
and see all the way to the front.
"What are we having for lunch, Alice?"

When her class
went to the zoo
all the children wanted
to sit by Alice on the bus
and be her partner.

Because Alice could reach up
and touch the bird cage
to make the birds sing
and see over the wall
to count the baby bears.

And when they had ice cream
the zooman always saw Alice first;
sometimes he gave her seconds,
and Alice always shared.

Alice could swim the length of the pool
while her friends were swimming across.

"I am SO lucky," Alice said, "to be too tall."

But soon Alice grew taller than the teachers,
taller than all the sixth grade,
and she was only in the fourth.

Then she grew taller even than the PRINCIPAL.

"No, Alice. You cannot be the princess –
We do not have a tall prince.
You may be the witch."
Alice was such a tall and s-c-a-r-r-y witch,
no one noticed the prince and the princess.
"Too Tall," the children said, "you were a real witch."

But Alice could not find
any jeans or sleeves long enough.
She could not turn cartwheels or be a cheerleader.

I am not so lucky to be Too Tall," Alice said.

So one day her mother picked her up at school
and took her to see Dr. Willoughby.
"Hello, Alice," Dr. Willoughby said.
"My, how you have grown."

"They call me Too Tall Alice at school," Alice said.

So, Dr. Willoughby measured her
and weighed her and typed on his computer and said,
"Alice, I can stop you from growing."

"Oh no," Alice said.
"Someone else would have to be Too Tall.
Who would I be? I want to be Me.
I want to be Too Tall."

So, Dr. Willoughby hugged Alice,
and her mother took her back to school.
"Hi, Too Tall," the children said.

"Hi," Alice said, smiling down at them.